A Celebration of Beatrix Potter

Art and Letters

by more than 30
of today's favorite
children's book
illustrators

FREDERICK WARNE & CO.
An Imprint of Penguin Random House

FREDERICK WARNE

Penguin Young Readers Group

An Imprint of Penguin Random House LLC

Penguin supports copyright. Copyright fuels creativity, encourages diverse voices, promotes free speech, and creates a vibrant culture.

Thank you for buying an authorized edition of this book and for complying with copyright laws by not reproducing, scanning,

or distributing any part of it in any form without permission. You are supporting writers and allowing Penguin to continue to publish books for every reader.

The copyright to the individual textual and visual selections are owned jointly by Frederick Warne & Co. and the respective contributors. Original copyright in text and illustrations © 1902 (*The Tale of Peter Rabbit*), 1903 (*The Tale of Squirrel Nutkin*; *The Tailor of Gloucester*), 1904 (*The Tale of Two Bad Mice*), 1905 (*The Tale of Mrs. Tiggy-Winkle*; *The Tale of The Pie and The Patty-Pan*), 1906 (*The Tale of Mr. Jeremy Fisher*), 1908 (*The Tale of Jemima Puddle-Duck*), and 1912 (*The Tale of Mr. Tod*) by Frederick Warne & Co. New reproductions copyright © 2002 by Frederick Warne & Co.

Beatrix Potter™ Frederick Warne & Co. Frederick Warne & Co. is the owner of all rights, copyrights, and trademarks in the Beatrix Potter character names and illustrations.

Designed and Art Directed by Giuseppe Castellano

Published in 2016 by Frederick Warne, an imprint of Penguin Random House LLC, 345 Hudson Street, New York, New York 10014. Manufactured in China.

ISBN 9780241249437 | 10 9 8 7 6 5 4 3 2 1

CONTENTS

ABOUT BEATRIX POTTER

Beatrix Potter is one of the most admired and inspirational children's book author-illustrators of all time.

Born in 1866, Beatrix grew up in the Victorian era—a time in which young women of wealth were expected to follow rigid societal strictures. From a young age, Potter had two interests: art and nature. She studied and sketched plants and animals, including rabbits, squirrels, mice, frogs, cats, hedgehogs, spores, and fungi.

Her parents' disapproval notwithstanding, Potter's fierce independence and unwavering curiosity led her to become a cryptographer, an amateur scientist, an award-winning farmer, a political activist, a revolutionary conservationist, and a forward-thinking businesswoman.

Potter's mastery of cadence and exquisite illustrations would lead her to be the beloved author-illustrator we all know today. Her books include:

ABOUT THIS BOOK

With the publication of her first book, Beatrix Potter changed the world of children's literature forever. Since 1902, Potter's oeuvre has influenced generations of authors and illustrators, intertwining her legacy into their own.

To celebrate the 150th anniversary of Potter's birth, thirty-two of today's favorite children's book author-illustrators share what she has meant to them. Inspired by their favorite tales and characters, these notable and award-winning artists reinterpret Potter's world in new and exciting ways.

Introductions of the tales in this book—*Peter Rabbit, Squirrel Nutkin, The Tailor of Gloucester, Two Bad Mice, Mrs. Tiggy Winkle, The Pie and The Patty Pan, Mr. Jeremy Fisher, Jemima Puddle-Duck*, and *Mr. Tod*—are presented in chronological order by publication date alongside her original illustrations.

This tribute, we hope, will serve not only as a way to honor Beatrix Potter, but also as a source of inspiration for future generations of authors and illustrators.

Thank you for joining us as we celebrate the amazing storyteller Beatrix Potter.

—The Stewards of Frederick Warne & Co.

Melissa Sweet

"It is all the same, drawing, painting, modeling, the irresistible desire to copy any beautiful object which strikes the eye. Why cannot one be content to look at it? I cannot rest, I must draw."—Beatrix Potter

Beatrix Potter was a naturalist from the age of nine. She grew up at a time when cataloging and recording the natural world merged art and science. Potter kept pet lizards, newts, snails, rabbits, and mice, and drew them as they moved, slept, and sat. In her stories we meet Flopsy, Mopsy, and Cotton–tail, as well as scientifically rendered mosses, flora, fauna, and fungi.

Potter's passion for observation led her to studying lichens under a microscope. She discovered that lichen was not (as previously thought) just an alga, but was both an alga and a fungi living together in a symbiotic relationship. As she was an untrained scientist and a woman, the scientific community didn't take her discovery seriously. She was discouraged but not deterred. Five years later, she self-published *The Tale of Peter Rabbit*. Her accurate renderings make her miniature worlds plausible—Peter Rabbit's tiny red slippers could fit only a rabbit's foot, the lettuces are as big as the rabbits, and mice hide under teacups. In response to Kenneth Grahame's *The Wind in the Willows* when Mr. Toad combs his hair, Potter wrote, "All writers for children ought to have a sufficient recognition of what things look like."

Beatrix Potter's art reminds us that the essence of good drawing is drawn from life.

NOW OF ALL IMPOSSIBLE THINGS TO DRAW...

The VERY WORST IS A FINE FAT FUNGUS.

FROM	JOURNAL
DATE	OCTOBER, 1892

The Tale of Peter Rabbit

1902

ABOUT THIS BOOK

The story of naughty Peter Rabbit in Mr. McGregor's garden first appeared in a picture letter Beatrix Potter wrote to Noel Moore, the young son of her former governess, in 1893. Encouraged by her success in having some greeting-card designs published, Beatrix remembered the letter seven years later, and expanded it into a little picture book, with black-and-white illustrations. It was rejected by several publishers, so Beatrix had it printed herself, to give to family and friends.

About this time, Frederick Warne agreed to publish the tale if the author would supply color pictures, and the book finally appeared in 1902, priced at one shilling. It was an instant success, and has remained so ever since. It has a pacy story with an engaging hero, an exciting chase, and a happy ending, matched with exquisite illustrations, and the result is a children's classic whose appeal is ageless.

Once upon a time there were four little Rabbits, and their names were —

Flopsy,

Mopsy,

Cotton-tail,

and Peter.

They lived with their Mother in a sand-bank, underneath the root of a very big fir-tree.

"Now, my dears," said old Mrs. Rabbit one morning, "you may go into the fields or down the lane, but don't go into Mr. McGregor's garden.

"Your Father had an accident there; he was put in a pie by Mrs. McGregor.

"Now run along, and don't get into mischief. I am going out."

Then old Mrs. Rabbit took a basket and her umbrella, and went through the wood to the baker's. She bought a loaf of brown bread and five currant buns.

Flopsy, Mopsy and Cotton-tail, who were good little bunnies, went down the lane to gather blackberries;

But Peter, who was very
naughty, ran straight away
to Mr. McGregor's garden,

And squeezed under the gate!

First he ate some lettuces
and some French beans; and
then he ate some radishes;

And then, feeling rather sick, he went to look for some parsley.

But round the end of a cucumber frame, whom should he meet but Mr. McGregor!

Mr. McGregor was on his hands and knees planting out young cabbages, but he jumped up and ran after Peter, waving a rake and calling out, "Stop thief!"

Mr. McGregor was quite sure that Peter was somewhere in the tool-shed, perhaps hidden underneath a flower-pot. He began to turn them over carefully, looking under each. Presently Peter sneezed — "Kertyschoo!" Mr. McGregor was after him in no time,

And tried to put his foot upon Peter, who jumped out of a window, upsetting three plants. The window was too small for Mr. McGregor, and he was tired of running after Peter. He went back to his work.

Peter sat down to rest; he was out of breath and trembling with fright, and he had not the least idea which way to go. Also he was very damp with sitting in that can.

After a time he began to wander about, going lippity — lippity — not very fast, and looking all round.
He found a door in a wall; but it was locked, and there was no room for a fat little rabbit to squeeze underneath.

Peter H. Reynolds

My mum, who was born in London (as was Beatrix Potter!), gave me a copy of *The Tale of Peter Rabbit* when I was a young boy. I loved the watercolor illustrations and the small size of the book, and, of course, I was certain that I had some connection to this bunny named Peter. Perhaps we were related somehow. I could certainly relate to his curiosity-fueled mischievousness. I remember being truly panicked when Mr. McGregor was after him and felt badly for this naked, terrified, naughty bunny. When he got home—finally—he was put to bed with some medicinal tea. I always felt sad that poor Peter didn't get the *best* medicine: his mama's hug. I have a chance now to share that scene.

Laura Vaccaro Seeger

The tales of Peter Rabbit were childhood favorites of mine, and though like many children I related to the mischievous Peter and his adventurous, impetuous nature, my favorite character was old Mrs. Rabbit.

Even as a young child, I was in awe of her. She had suffered a terrible loss (her husband had become the main ingredient in Mrs. McGregor's pie!) and still she remained productive, optimistic, and loving as she raised her four bunny children. She understood the need for independence and she made certain that while they must learn from experience, they always had a safe home to return to.

She was, in many ways, much like my own mother. For example, upon discovering that I had taken a pair of scissors to all my mother's fine jewelry in order to make golden glitter for my collage "masterpiece," she sent me to bed with the equivalent of Mrs. Rabbit's chamomile tea, and was at once appropriately angry and supportively understanding. It is with such nurturing that creativity is able to flourish.

Beatrix Potter understood creativity, and was masterful at creating a juxtaposition of reality and fantasy, emotion and human frailties. With few words and beautifully painted pictures, she managed to convey innocence, fear, courage, wisdom, love, and so much more.

Brian Pinkney

When I was a kid, I loved Beatrix Potter's illustrations of Peter Rabbit! They were such a playful depiction of Peter's personality, and they always sparked my imagination.

While growing up in Boston, I often imagined Peter scurrying about the streets. He had a special way of appearing at the playground and during my walk to school. In my kid's-eye view, Peter was like a boy in a rabbit's body. He was curious and adventuresome in a world of grown-ups who were clueless about his presence, in my mind's eye. Blue has always been my favorite color, so I have always loved Peter's blue jacket. Back then, it was as if Peter and I had our own color-buddy friendship! Now, as an adult, I imagine Peter Rabbit scurrying around having a ball in Clinton Hill, Brooklyn, where I live.

Brendan Wenzel

For any child like myself, who spent almost all their time outside, Beatrix Potter's world was a gift. Carrying her characters and stories with me as I tromped off into the forest allowed a young explorer to infuse every hollow and thicket with possibility and magic, but perhaps just as importantly, with familiarity. With Jeremy Fisher and Peter Rabbit somewhere out there in the world, a kid like me felt braver testing those limits and wandering a bit farther from home.

But while her more charming creations worked to make the world a bit less frightening, her great villain cast his wide bespectacled shadow over those places most familiar. What a brilliant move for Potter to forgo wild-eyed wolves and sinister serpents and to instead give her ominous dark force a white picket fence and a quaint little garden right downtown. Mr. McGregor: Could there be a more terrifying concept to a young adventurer? For where the dark denizens of most stories quickly seem to find themselves being chased from villages with pitchforks, or at least properly labeled as fiends, McGregor's claim to his garden, his brutality in the defense of produce, enabled his awful deeds to go unpunished.

For me, this made the bearded beast a near perfect bogeyman; the thought of his cold gaze, meaty hands, and razor-sharp rake snuffed out any mischievous thought that might pop into my head. McGregor's warning was simple: Wander outside the borders, cross any of those carefully drawn lines, and you will end up in a pie. Potter was a genius, and I have never trespassed.

E. B. Lewis

I was first introduced to Beatrix Potter's work as a child, long before I even thought I was an artist. I remember sitting on my living room floor staring at the images in that tiny green book. The characters were simple, beautiful, and full of life. They seemed to tell their own story. I know without a doubt Beatrix has influenced my work. She repeatedly said, "the shorter and the plainer, the better," which is the focus of my art. Beatrix Potter remains one of my favorite illustrators.

Betsy Lewin

Beatrix Potter's book *The Tale of Peter Rabbit* was among my favorite picture books when I was a child. I've always been fond of animals, and I love the warm, endearing personalities she gave her characters. Peter Rabbit was my favorite because, like me, he was mischievous and adventuresome, sometimes finding himself in hot water.

When I grew up, I became more interested in Beatrix Potter. She was a shining example of a woman making a place for herself as an artist and author in the world of publishing at a time in history when it must have seemed all but impossible. In the 1950s it seemed all but impossible to me, but I jumped in with both feet and am both thankful and still a bit surprised that I didn't drown.

Chris Haughton

I remember being quite shocked by the page in *The Tale of Peter Rabbit* where Father Rabbit got put into a pie. When Peter Rabbit runs straight to Mr. McGregor's garden, I vividly remember willing him not to go. I think I was quite cautious as a young child and I couldn't understand why on earth he wanted to go in there at all. The blackberries outside the garden looked a lot tastier than the vegetables, anyway.

As an adult, I was fascinated to learn about Beatrix Potter herself. Her love for the natural world and her awareness of the need for its conservation were many, many decades ahead of her time. Even without her books, her beautiful botanical and mycological illustrations and scientific studies alone would have made her a remarkable female figure in Victorian times. Her stories and images could only have come from a lifetime of keenly drawing and observing animals and wildlife.

David Ezra Stein

My son is a picky eater. If I want him to eat his mashed potatoes, I pretend to be Mr. McGregor from *The Tale of Peter Rabbit*. I flatten his potatoes into a "sidewalk" and, in a poor imitation of a Scottish accent, ask him to keep an eye on my new sidewalk for me for a while. Of course, as soon as I turn away, he mischievously snaps up a bite of potato. I feign outrage, but never realize who the culprit is, and he plays innocent. We go on like this until all the mashed potatoes are gone.

McGregor also appears in another game, with me in the villain's role, of course. My kids, two and five, sneak into my "garden" (some pillows, or a table, or wherever we happen to be) and steal vegetables, only to have me shout, "Rabbits!" and chase them back into their imaginary burrows. It's endlessly fun. They are filled with fear and daring, sneaking into the garden again and again.

These games of chase and trickery, and the desire to outsmart the oaflike grown-up, are quintessential to a child's outlook and development. As a writer, Beatrix Potter seems to have known well the child's heart. And, along with her stunning artwork, her stories bring generations of children into her garden, over and over again.

Jon Agee

The Tale of Peter Rabbit is a thriller—with a great villain: Mr. McGregor. McGregor has already eaten up Peter's father in a pie, so the thought of him catching Peter kept me riveted to my seat as my mom read the book. The most anxious moment came when Peter was cornered in the toolshed. There was something strangely adorable and terrifying about a rabbit hiding in a watering can, with his ears poking out of the top.

Kelly Murphy

The stomp of a boot. The drag of the rake. The pie in the oven. Mr. McGregor is seldom seen but ever-present, lurking at every page turn. In the first Beatrix Potter tale, it is revealed that Peter Rabbit's father had been killed by Mr. McGregor. Country life can be rather dreadful to creatures both big and small.

Potter's charming artwork and delightful language become even more powerful because of the tragic backdrop of farm life. With darling waistcoats and pert eyes, she can weave a captivating tale filled with real-life theatrics. Potter shows us that while there can be excitement and mischief, it is quick wit and keen eyes that are needed for living another day!

Backyard birding is one of my favorite pastimes, and as every birder knows, squirrels are the bane of our existence. I sometimes yell, shout, and even throw things at the nuisances in my yard. After my ridiculous display, I remember the vivid world of Beatrix Potter and realize that somewhere behind a tree, the animals are laughing at me.

Jarrett J. Krosoczka

When I look at the illustrations in Beatrix Potter's books, I marvel at the quality of the anatomy in her animals.

She was working in the early 1900s, and it's clear that she drew from reference.

Ms. Potter was an enthusiastic naturalist, and this is apparent in her work.

As a young girl, she and her brother would draw the small animals they kept as pets.

Starting at age fourteen, Ms. Potter kept a journal, oftentimes drawing the world around her.

She studied natural science and botany, drawing and painting items from nature and taxidermic animals.

She spent her adult years on a farm, surrounding herself with creatures that offered her frequent inspiration.

And what do I do when I need visual reference for a character? I look up photos online. How lazy.

I need to remember to be more like Beatrix Potter and draw from the wildlife that surrounds me...

The Tale of Squirrel Nutkin

1903

ABOUT THIS BOOK

In 1901, Beatrix Potter was spending the summer with her family in the Lake District. She wrote a letter all about the squirrels she saw there to eight-year-old Norah Moore, the daughter of her former governess: "An old lady who lives on the island says she thinks they come over the lake when her nuts are ripe; but I wonder how they can get across the water? Perhaps they make little rafts!" The letter then goes on to tell the story of Nutkin, the cheeky squirrel who is finally punished by Old Brown, an owl whom Beatrix has substituted for the old lady of her letter.

RIDDLES FROM THE TALE OF SQUIRREL NUTKIN

In this story, Nutkin taunts Old Brown with his riddles:

"Riddle me, riddle me, rot-tot-tote!
A little wee man, in a red red coat!
A staff in his hand, and a stone in
    his throat;
If you'll tell me this riddle, I'll give
    you a groat." [1]

"Old Mr. B! Riddle-me-ree!
Hitty Pitty within the wall,
Hitty Pitty without the wall;
If you touch Hitty Pitty,
Hitty Pitty will bite you!" [2]

"The man in the wilderness
   said to me,
'How many strawberries grow
   in the sea?'
I answered him as I thought
   good —
'As many red herrings as grow
   in the wood.'"

"Old Mr. B! Riddle-me-ree!
Flour of England, fruit of Spain,
Met together in a shower of rain;
Put in a bag tied round with a string,
If you'll tell me this riddle, I'll give
   you a ring!" [3]

1. A cherry; 2. A nettle; 3. Plum pudding

David Soman

It's not a question I ever asked when I was young and poring over Beatrix Potter stories, but now I wonder: How did she do it? How could she make up stories and pictures that were filled with so many contradictory things at once? How did she make worlds that are cozy and sweet, yet often filled with terrible life-and-death danger? How did she draw animals realistically and yet convince me that they lived in houses and wore clothes, though sometimes they didn't? How did she make her particularly English countryside of the nineteenth century feel normal to a boy growing up in 1970s New York City (and how come I still feel that that is how the world is *supposed* to look)? And then *the names*? How did she come up with these incredible names? I mean, what is better than Squirrel Nutkin? How did she fit the whole, big, complicated, contradictory world into the palm of my hands and then into the hands of my daughter and sons? How did she do it? Thinking about that now, I think there is only one answer.

It was magic.

The Tailor of
Gloucester
1903

ABOUT THIS BOOK

The Tailor of Gloucester was Beatrix Potter's own favorite among all her books. She first heard the true story on which it is based when visiting her cousin, Caroline Hutton, who lived near Gloucester. Leaving an unfinished waistcoat for the mayor of Gloucester in his shop one Saturday morning, a tailor was amazed to find it ready on Monday, except for one buttonhole, for which there was "no more twist." In reality, his two assistants had secretly completed the job, but Beatrix Potter has the work finished by little brown mice. She adds an extra note of enchantment by setting the story on Christmas Eve, when animals can talk, and weaving in many of her favorite traditional rhymes.

Four-and-twenty tailors
Went to catch a snail,
The best man amongst them
Durst not touch her tail;
She put out her horns
Like a little kyloe cow,
Run, tailors, run or she'll
 have you all e'en now!
Sieve my lady's oatmeal,
Grind my lady's flour,
Put it in a chestnut,
Let it stand an hour —

Three little mice sat down to spin,
Pussy passed by and she peeped in.
What are you at, my fine little men?
Making coats for gentlemen.
Shall I come in and cut off your
    threads?
Oh, no, Miss Pussy, you'd bite off
    our heads!
Hey diddle dinketty, poppetty pet!
The merchants of London they
    wear scarlet;
Silk in the collar, and gold in the hem,
So merrily march the merchantmen!

G. Brian Karas

I have to confess, I came to read *The Tailor of Gloucester* for the first time quite late in life. (It was right after I was asked to contribute to this book.) It wasn't a lack of interest that kept me away. I read and reread many Beatrix Potter stories at bedtime with my two young sons. We all looked forward to the tales of Peter Rabbit, Mrs. Tiggy-winkle, Benjamin Bunny, and Two Bad Mice, all perfect little stories for drifting off to sleep. And that was the problem—we were all asleep, or close to it, by the time we got to the much longer *The Tailor of Gloucester*. If there happened to be time for one more story, we (I!) would opt for something shorter. And now that I've finally read what the author regarded as her own favorite story, I see what we have missed. It would have been a favorite of ours, too. My sons would have urged on the tired tailor, laughed at outsmarted Simpkin, and cheered for the industrious and sartorial mice. And afterward, they might have wondered at whether it was possible for mice to really do such a thing. That's what I love about Beatrix Potter's work. Her stories could, with the smallest amount of imagination, be real.

Rosemary Wells

I remember being eight. I can see the slope of my own knees under the blanket on days when I was ill and could not go to school. On those occasions I would ask for all the Potter books at once and read them in succession. The little bunny on the rocking horse is a good example of how profoundly her work influenced me to choose small animals as characters.

She has also given me just as much with her written words, because she was also a superb and precise writer.

Beatrix Potter brought a complete emotional range, common sense, and common morality to her set of English hedgerow animals. She did this in much the same effortless way Glenn Gould played Bach.

Years later, in preparation for the Mother Goose books, I was invited to spend many hours in the collection vaults of the Victoria and Albert Museum in London, curator Anne Hobbs at my side. I held the precious B. P. watercolors, studied them, and drank them in with my eyes. I remember the weight of her paper in my hand, and never getting quite enough.

As I look at the beloved books, now in my granddaughters' library, I hear my mother's voice, crisp and gentle, reading *The Tailor of Gloucester* aloud. The words are as perfect and unassuming as the drawings themselves. B. P. was as great a genius writer as she was a watercolorist. She was the first stellar children's storyteller in the English language.

R Wells

The Tale of Two Bad Mice
1904

ABOUT THIS BOOK

The Tale of Two Bad Mice was written at a particularly happy time for Beatrix Potter—she and her editor, Norman Warne, were becoming close friends, and Beatrix was sometimes included in Warne family celebrations. Norman made a new cage for Beatrix's pet mice, Tom Thumb and Hunca Munca, so that she could more easily draw them for her new book. He had also made a dollhouse for his favorite niece, Winifred, and Beatrix was invited to visit and sketch this, too. However, her mother objected, and so Beatrix had to make do with photographs and examples of doll's furniture and food that Norman sent her. She kept some of the furniture all her life, and it can still be seen at Hill Top, her first Lakeland home.

One morning Lucinda and Jane had gone out for a drive in the doll's perambulator. There was no one in the nursery, and it was very quiet. Presently there was a little scuffling, scratching noise in a corner near the fire-place, where there was a hole under the skirting-board.

Tom Thumb put out his head for a moment, and then popped it in again.

Tom Thumb was a mouse.

A minute afterwards, Hunca Munca, his wife, put her head out, too; and when she saw that there was no one in the nursery, she ventured out on the oilcloth under the coal-box.

The doll's-house stood at the other side of the fire-place. Tom Thumb and Hunca Munca went cautiously across the hearthrug. They pushed the front door — it was not fast.

Tom Thumb and Hunca Munca went upstairs and peeped into the dining-room. Then they squeaked with joy!

Such a lovely dinner was laid out upon the table! There were tin spoons, and lead knives and forks, and two dolly-chairs — all *so* convenient!

Wendell Minor

My mother always loved Beatrix Potter stories, and delighted in sharing them with me and with her nursery school children for thirty-five years.

I loved *The Tale of Peter Rabbit* and *The Tale of Two Bad Mice* because I was always getting into trouble throughout my childhood, doing things I was told not to do! I felt a kinship with Peter and the mice. They gave me the feeling that we were partners in mischief, breaking down barriers and exploring new worlds. It was all a great adventure to me.

Later in life, as I developed as an artist, I became more interested in the person behind all of these wonderful animal tales. Potter's scientific studies of nature's many creatures and landscape drawings and watercolors come from the observant eye of a fine artist. Her in-depth scrutiny of the natural world has given children a treasury of wonderful and imaginary animal tales that will remain timeless for generations to come.

My illustration *The Troublemakers Meet* imagines my favorite characters meeting by chance and planning a new and mischievous adventure in Beatrix Potter's world.

Jen Corace

Three things come to mind when I think of Hunca Munca.

One, Hunca Munca is a name that is the exact opposite of Jennifer or Jen. Which is not to say that I dislike my name, but if you grew up in the seventies and eighties and were named Jennifer . . . you most likely daydreamed of exotic names like Jody or Samantha. Hunca Munca takes the cake.

Two, I grew up around dollhouses. My grandmother had a particular love of them. She had a built-in corner china cabinet whose bottom half was converted into a three-floor dollhouse. I loved it. I loved that corner of the house and spending hours working out stories, mostly about murder. It was a dangerous dollhouse.

My own dollhouse I received at Christmas, at about the age of five. My mom, who was a decorator to her very core, painstakingly painted and wallpapered the entire structure. She made rugs out of scraps of fabric, sewed curtains for the windows, and framed small pictures in balsa wood for the walls. This dollhouse was less about murder and more about ghosts. It was *very* haunted.

Three, the disappointment Hunca Munca feels after she finds the red and blue beads in the canisters that promised coffee, rice, and sago . . . I get it. I've been there. We all have. Expectation and disappointment are difficult experiences to balance, and it's sometimes tricky to manage our reaction. It's stories like these and characters like Hunca Munca that can give us a little vicarious release. So thank you, Hunca Munca.

Peggy Rathmann

Beatrix Potter's mother allowed her daughter to keep a small zoo in her nursery. My mother, hoping that pet rodents were the key to Beatrix Potter's success, let the five of us keep all the mice, rats, and guinea pigs we wanted.

Results were mixed. Several of us developed mouse phobias.

Mom and I, however, are still fans of Hunca Munca, the lovely mouse who stars with her husband in *The Tale of Two Bad Mice*. In fact, our only issue with the book is its title: How could such a sweet mother mouse be "bad"?

Here is Hunca Munca with her children at a dollhouse birthday party.

Uh-oh . . .

The Tale of Mrs. Tiggy-Winkle

1905

ABOUT THIS BOOK

Although many of Beatrix Potter's storybook animals were based on her own pets, she often gave them human qualities, too. The character of Mrs. Tiggy-winkle was inspired by Kitty MacDonald, an old Scottish washerwoman who was "a comical, round little old woman, as brown as a berry and wears a multitude of petticoats." Beatrix's tame hedgehog, Mrs. Tiggy-winkle, was a model: "So long as she can go to sleep on my knee she is delighted, but if she is propped up on end for half an hour, she first begins to yawn pathetically, and then she *does* bite! Nevertheless she is a dear person."

Then away down the hill trotted Lucie and Mrs. Tiggy-winkle with the bundles of clothes!

All the way down the path little animals came out of the fern to meet them; the very first that they met were Peter Rabbit and Benjamin Bunny!

And she gave them their nice clean clothes; and all the little animals and birds were so very much obliged to dear Mrs. Tiggy-winkle.

So that at the bottom of
the hill when they came to
the stile, there was nothing
left to carry except Lucie's
one little bundle.

Lucie scrambled up the stile
with the bundle in her hand;
and then she turned to say
"Good-night," and to thank
the washer-woman. —
But what a *very* odd thing!
Mrs. Tiggy-winkle had not
waited either for thanks or
for the washing bill!

She was running running
running up the hill — and
where was her white frilled
cap? and her shawl? and her
gown — and her petticoat?

Tomie dePaola

I didn't know that a lady named Beatrix Potter wrote the story of Peter Rabbit (and drew the pictures for it, too) until years after the book was first read to me. I liked the story. I liked the naughty bunny who went into the garden when he wasn't supposed to. I liked his dangerous adventure and I liked that he was given this strange stuff called chamomile tea, instead of plain old blackberries, at the end of the book.

When I discovered the real Beatrix Potter, it was at the Victoria and Albert Museum in London, years later. They had mounted a show of her botanical drawings. Miss Potter was indeed more than the lady who painted naughty bunnies.

Then she married and became Mrs. Heelis—even more interesting, with her love of Herdwick sheep and conserving the landscape and farms of the Lake District in England.

And I love that the older Mrs. Heelis began to resemble the lovely, slightly cranky Mrs. Tiggy-winkle, the hedgehog laundress that Miss Potter had drawn years earlier.

So, may I present: Mrs. Heelis and Mrs. Tiggy-winkle having tea when Mrs. Tiggy-winkle brought the laundry.

There's a book idea!

Stephanie Graegin

It was the small size of Beatrix Potter's books that initially drew me to them.

In my tiny hands, they seemed custom-made for me—I should say I was four years old at the time. Potter managed to create a world full of memorable characters that were endlessly fascinating and naturalistic. In her world, you could experience mortal danger, like your father being baked in a pie or your tail being taken off by an owl. You could also be comforted by good little rabbits having blackberries and milk for dinner, or a friendly hedgehog ironing your handkerchief. Few children's writers have created a world like hers: sweet, dark, comforting, and a bit scary at times.

During my first interactions with Potter's books, I wasn't quite old enough to read on my own, but I pored over her drawings and ingested them, which pushed me to try and create my own. With crayons and typing paper, I would sit at the kitchen table and draw countless little animals, all wearing little shirts, jackets, dresses, and other human accoutrements. I could never have imagined my youthful admiration for her drawings and stories would provide me with my own avenues of expression as an adult. As a burgeoning art student, I created all manner of storybook characters, but as I've matured as an artist, I have circled around to what are quintessentially my roots—the wellspring that is Beatrix Potter.

The Tale of The Pie and The Patty-Pan

1905

ABOUT THIS BOOK

This story was originally written in 1903, then put aside until 1905. The tale reflects Beatrix's affection for the Lake District village of Sawrey and its inhabitants, and was one she was particularly pleased with: "If the book prints well it will be my next favorite to *The Tailor*."

She put on a lilac silk gown, for the party, and an embroidered muslin apron and tippet.

"It is very strange," said Ribby, "I did not *think* I left that drawer pulled out; has somebody been trying on my mittens?"

She came downstairs again, and made the tea, and put the teapot on

the hob. She peeped again into the *bottom* oven; the pie had become a lovely brown, and it was steaming hot.

She sat down before the fire to wait for the little dog. "I am glad I used the *bottom* oven," said Ribby, "the top one would certainly have been very much too hot. I wonder why that cupboard door was open? Can there really have been someone in the house?"

Very punctually at four o'clock, Duchess started to go to the party. She ran so fast through the village that she was too early, and she had to wait a little while in the lane that leads down to Ribby's house.

"I wonder if Ribby has taken *my* pie out of the oven yet?" said Duchess, "and whatever can have become of the other pie made of mouse?"

At a quarter past four to the minute, there came a most genteel little tap-tappity. "Is Mrs. Ribston at home?" inquired Duchess in the porch.

"Come in! and how do you do? my dear Duchess," cried Ribby. "I hope I see you well?"

"Quite well, I thank you, and how do *you* do, my dear Ribby?" said Duchess. "I've brought you some flowers; what a delicious smell of pie!"

"Oh, what lovely flowers! Yes, it is mouse and bacon!"

"Do not talk about food, my dear Ribby," said Duchess; "what a lovely white tea-cloth! . . . Is it done to a turn? Is it still in the oven?"

"I think it wants another five minutes," said Ribby. "Just a shade longer; I will pour out the tea, while we wait. Do you take sugar, my dear Duchess?"

Renata Liwska

I admit I was one of those kids (and adults) who mostly looks at the pictures. And this is doubly true with the wonderful pictures Beatrix Potter made. So when I approached this project, I went back and read through a bunch of her stories. *The Tale of The Pie and The Patty-Pan* is the one I identified with the most—mostly because I can see a lot of myself in the character Duchess. Even after some Web searching, I am not really sure what a patty-pan is, but I'm afraid to say I could very much feel the anxieties and fears that led to Duchess potentially swallowing one.

Another reason this story touched me is the extraordinarily adorable drawings of Duchess by Miss Potter! The ink drawing of the little dog brushing her black coat makes me smile and fills me with joy every time I see it. But when I went to draw, I was more than a bit intimidated. In such situations, I find it is best to let my pencil lead the way and trust it will find the right drawing for me. And so it led me to draw Dr. Maggotty, the magpie doctor that Ribby called on to help Duchess. I am not sure if it was the "alacrity" of how Miss Potter captured the character of magpies, or that I have been watching the antics of a magpie on my balcony lately, but Mr. Maggotty made me smile and so I just had to draw him, with a bit of a modern take.

The Tale of Mr. Jeremy Fisher

1906

ABOUT THIS BOOK

Mr. Jeremy Fisher had existed in Beatrix Potter's imagination for many years before his story was eventually published in 1906. He first appeared in 1893 in a picture letter to Eric Moore, written by Beatrix the day after she had sent the Peter Rabbit story to his brother Noel. In 1894, she produced a series of black-and-white frog drawings, which were published in a children's annual, and in 1902, Beatrix discussed Mr. Jeremy with her editor, Norman Warne. After Norman's death in 1905, Beatrix needed to work and took up the story with Harold, Norman's brother, as her new editor. "I feel as if my work and your kindness will be my greatest comfort." Perhaps the solitary hours spent sketching tranquil scenes in the Lake District did bring Beatrix comfort: the book certainly contains some of her most beautiful paintings.

Once upon a time there was a frog called Mr. Jeremy Fisher; he lived in a little damp house amongst the buttercups at the edge of a pond.

The water was all slippy-sloppy in the larder and in the back passage.

But Mr. Jeremy liked getting his feet wet, nobody ever scolded him, and he never caught a cold!

He was quite pleased when he looked out and saw large drops of rain, splashing in the pond —

"I will get some worms and go fishing and catch a dish of minnows for my dinner," said Mr. Jeremy Fisher. "If I catch more than five fish, I will invite my friends Mr. Alderman Ptolemy Tortoise and Sir Isaac Newton. The Alderman, however, eats salad."

Mr. Jeremy put on a macintosh, and a pair of shiny goloshes;

he took his rod and basket, and set off with enormous hops to the place where he kept his boat.

The boat was round and green, and very like the other lily-leaves. It was tied to a water-plant in the middle of the pond.

Tony DiTerlizzi

From the woods beyond Mr. McGregor's garden to a secret hillside door that opens into the home of Mrs. Tiggy-winkle, the storied forests of Beatrix Potter's imagination are a place I have visited time and time again since childhood.

Her inhabitants are the familiar faces of rabbits, cats, ducks, mice, and frogs—each transmogrified into living, speaking characters, uniquely attired to fit their personalities. Though this menagerie sounds typical for your average nursery story, Potter's artwork sidesteps the saccharine for a studied—nay scientific—stroll through a woodsy world filled with mischief, peril, and consequence.

So deep was my yearning to explore beyond the boundaries of her pages that I returned to *The Tale of Mr. Jeremy Fisher* in hopes of discovering an image not seen in Potter's original book. With my imagination fully submerged into her watercolor realm I asked the amphibious angler where he'd acquired gear and tackle. Thereupon he led me to a ramshackle bait shop, run by an affable water rat. With pencils and paintbrush in hand, I conjured Potter's spirit to capture the scene as best I could.

Upon returning to Mr. Fisher's dampish home we were joined by Sir Isaac Newton and Mr. Alderman Ptolemy Tortoise. I shared my sketches with them over a meal of roasted grasshopper in ladybird sauce. They approved, and we raised our glasses to fine art, fine company, and a good life. Best of all, we toasted the magnificence of Beatrix Potter.

Chuck Groenink

What I remember best about Beatrix Potter's stories are all the fantastically cozy little homes she gave her characters—from Jeremy Fisher's splishy-splashy little cottage by the water to the mice hidden away under the floorboards decorating their rooms with stolen furniture from dollhouses. Each had a perfect little space of his or her own. Reading those stories, there was nothing I wanted more than to be able to visit all those abodes.

Dan Santat

Jeremy is the average hardworking middle-class man. He decides to go fishing and declares that if he catches more than five minnows he will invite his friends over for dinner and share the joy of his bounty. I identify with Jeremy as the people pleaser. He doesn't ask others to participate in his pursuit to organize the dinner, but rather, decides that if things go well, he will share in the joy of his success. In Jeremy's mind, the copacetic state of the Universe is the very reason to celebrate. It reminds me of the days back when I was a child and my parents would throw parties. It wasn't done to celebrate one's success or honor the annual celebration of a person growing a year older. It was done for the joy of being alive while being in the company of friends. Despite Mr. Fisher's failed attempt at acquiring the fish, he and his friends still manage to make the best of a situation by offering the alternative dish of roasted grasshopper while his friend, Mr. Alderman Ptolemy Tortoise, brings a salad for everyone to share. The beauty of the celebration isn't that it is fancy, but that it simply happened.

David Wiesner

The extraordinary quality of Beatrix Potter's work strikes you immediately. The combination of closely observed research and beautifully sensitive painting makes the characters leap off the page. The character shadings are incredibly subtle. All of her animals have their own personality. Potter didn't create those personalities by exaggerating faces or anatomy—they are real bunnies and kitties, and each one is an individual.

Jeremy Fisher is certainly an individual. With his jacket, waistcoat, and cravat, he exudes an elegant fussiness tinged with grandeur. He is also a perfectly observed, anatomically correct frog.

Except for his feet.

In all of Potter's other stories, I do not see another instance of her deviating from the true anatomy of the animal she is drawing, with the exception of adding opposable thumbs to paws.

And yet, look at Jeremy Fisher's feet. Those tiny, delicate shoes cannot possibly contain his frog feet. Midway through the story, his shoes come off in the water and there they are—great big, long-toed feet! Later, back on land, Jeremy has those little shoes on again.

It pleases me that for the sake of her story, Beatrix Potter chose characterization over anatomical accuracy.

"I found it last Tuesday. What do you think?"

The Tale of Jemima Puddle-Duck
1908

ABOUT THIS BOOK

Beatrix Potter's love of Hill Top and farming shine through this story. She painted her farm manager's wife, Mrs. Cannon, feeding the poultry, while the children, Ralph and Betsy (to whom this "farmyard tale" is dedicated), are also illustrated. Kep the collie was Beatrix's favorite sheepdog, and Jemima herself was a real duck that lived at Hill Top. She is a most popular character—self-important and naive, but very endearing.

Jemima Puddle-duck was not much in the habit of flying. She ran downhill a few yards flapping her shawl, and then she jumped off into the air.

She flew beautifully when she had got a good start.

She skimmed along over the tree-tops until she saw an open place in the middle of the wood, where the trees and brushwood had been cleared.

Jemima alighted rather heavily, and began to waddle about in search of a convenient dry nesting-place.

She rather fancied a tree-stump amongst some tall fox-gloves.

But — seated upon the stump, she was startled to find an elegantly dressed gentleman reading a newspaper.

He had black prick ears and sandy-coloured whiskers.

"Quack?" said Jemima Puddle-duck, with her head and her bonnet on one side — "Quack?"

The gentleman raised his eyes above his newspaper and looked curiously at Jemima —

"Madam, have you lost your way?" said he. He had a long bushy tail which he was sitting upon, as the stump was somewhat damp.

Jemima thought him mighty civil and handsome. She explained that she had not lost her way, but that she was trying to find a convenient dry nesting-place.

"Ah! is that so? indeed!" said the gentleman with sandy whiskers, looking curiously at Jemima. He folded up the newspaper, and put it in his coat-tail pocket.

Matthew Forsythe

We love Jemima because she is a duck who won't accept her station. She is impelled to live her own life and not give in to others' expectations. She is the Emma Bovary of children's literature.

Paul O. Zelinsky

I've always liked little things. So did Beatrix Potter: Mice and bugs, squirrels, and baby rabbits populate the tiny books she made. In her created world, the characters are part farmland animals and part English country folk. But the lives of these creatures are no safer than those of their real-life animal counterparts. If you're a rabbit, the farmer will try to catch and skin you for fur. If you're a duck, you risk being eaten. Beatrix Potter has no time for sentiment: Things are what they are and we must carry on with the story. Still, the small size of her books and the light touch of her watercolor illustrations somehow lighten the stakes. And her matter-of-fact tone in the face of animal disaster comes across, to me, as terribly funny, in a special, British way.

My favorite of her books is *The Tale of Jemima Puddle-Duck*. Jemima was a bad egg-sitter and a worse judge of character, but she had gumption and initiative and a lovely red shawl and a blue poke bonnet. It was her insistent nature that almost got her and her unborn children devoured by a fox. Jemima's life was saved by good luck and by smarter friends, and she didn't learn a thing from the whole experience.

So I thought I would take this drawing opportunity to give the poor duck something she never received in her own book, something she wouldn't have gotten in a real Beatrix Potter story. I've given her a cozy afternoon tea in the company of this friendly fox, who, because it's my drawing, can be kindly to the core and not like a real fox at all. May the many ducklings I added, the ones Jemima couldn't lay or save or rear in the book, bring her happiness.

Lauren Castillo

From day one, Beatrix Potter's characters were there to welcome me to the world. Her magical art graced the walls of my nursery room, and was the very first illustration my little eyes were exposed to. I can still remember the details of that wallpaper design with Jemima, Peter, Flopsy, Mopsy and Cotton-tail, and the comforting way it made me feel as I was drifting off to sleep at night, or waking up in the morning. Those special characters kept me company and were dear friends.

As a student studying illustration, and as a bookmaker today, I continue to look to and admire the work of Miss Potter and the charming world she created. It is warm and inviting, and stirs up so many happy childhood memories.

The Tale of Mr. Tod

1912

ABOUT THIS BOOK

With the publication of this story, Beatrix Potter claimed to be tired of writing "goody goody books about nice people." Her principal characters, Mr. Tod (the old Saxon name for a fox) and Tommy Brock (the country word for a badger), are indeed disagreeable, though their story has a happy ending.

I have made many books about well-behaved people. Now, for a change, I am going to make a story about two disagreeable people, called Tommy Brock and Mr. Tod.

Nobody could call Mr. Tod "nice". The rabbits could not bear him; they could smell him half a mile off. He was of a wandering habit and he had foxy whiskers; they never knew where he would be next.

One day he was living in a stick-house in the coppice, causing terror to the family of old Mr. Benjamin Bouncer. Next day he moved into a pollard willow near the lake, frightening the wild ducks and the water rats.

In winter and early spring he might generally be found in an earth amongst the rocks at the top of Bull Banks, under Oatmeal Crag.

He had half a dozen houses, but he was seldom at home.

The houses were not always empty when Mr. Tod moved *out*; because sometimes Tommy Brock moved *in*; (without asking leave).

Tommy Brock was a short bristly fat waddling person with a grin; he grinned all over his face. He was not nice in his habits. He ate wasp nests and frogs and worms; and he waddled about by moonlight, digging things up.

Judy Schachner

"Nobody could call Mr. Tod 'nice.' The rabbits could not bear him; they could smell him half a mile off."

I, on the other hand, adore the likes of Mr. Tod, one of Beatrix Potter's most "disagreeable" characters.

She wasn't all fluff and bunnies, you know. Though Beatrix Potter's illustrations were tame and pretty in their skilled portrayal of the natural world, her words would often hint at the somewhat darker truths of nature... Heck, they did more than hint, they were matter-of-fact honest.

Like when we come to the end of Jemima Puddle-duck's tale, Potter describes the demise of another fox using these words: "barking, baying, growls and howls, squealing and groans." Groans, no less! And just when we think we will never recover from the vision those words deposited in our sleepy little brains of a fox being torn to shreds by puppy hounds, Beatrix Potter goes one step further—by allowing those puppy hounds to eat Jemima Puddle-duck's eggs!

Oh, the horror!

Was it wrong those thirty years ago to have the bumpers in my baby girl's crib covered in the fabric of Beatrix Potter stories before I actually read them? I think so . . . and I'm pretty sure that Beatrix Potter would agree.

Pat Cummings

Having spent so much of my childhood abroad, I didn't encounter Beatrix Potter's stories until I was older. But when I did find her books, what struck me was the subtlety and sensitivity in Potter's drawings. Each character's clothes, demeanor . . . even their accessories reveal such careful and tender observation.

And then, neatly injected into all that soft sweetness that is her trademark, Potter introduced Mr. Tod, a roguish outlier who annoys, perplexes, and even frightens the other creatures. Mr. Tod is mysterious, dapper (if threadbare), and a bit unsavory, maybe, but confident of his ability to charm.

When he appears, the other animals must prick up their ears, sharpen their senses. Foxes are exceptionally handsome. And Mr. Tod is a delightful mix of catalyst, cad, and clever charmer . . . my kind of antihero. Ducks and bunnies notwithstanding, every story needs a bit of trouble.

Chris Raschka

How can you not like Tommy Brock? He is so thoroughly disagreeable. He goes to bed in his boots, smokes a cabbage-leaf cigar that stings your eyes, and eats rabbit babies when he gets ahold of them. Terrible! But in the nearly perfect world of Beatrix Potter, it is great fun to have a character like him. And Beatrix Potter introduces him so charmingly. Perfection is nice enough, but it can get a little boring.

Beatrix Potter was nearly perfect herself. But not quite. And that is why we still love her so.

TOMMY BROCK

He ate wasp nests
and frogs and worms;
and he waddled about
by moonlight, digging
things up.

EPILOGUE

*L*ater in life, Beatrix Potter was not able to walk in the wilderness she had grown to love.

"As I lie in bed," she wrote, *"I can walk step by step on the fells and rough land seeing every stone and flower and patch of bog and cotton pass where my old legs will never take me again."*

Potter died after her seventy-seventh birthday, leaving four thousand acres of land to the National Trust. But her legacy extends beyond the land she has protected: she immortalized the cottages and animals and the countryside in her timeless stories and beautiful art.

Every year, more than two million of Beatrix Potter's books are sold worldwide. Her legacy, much like her life, extends from the English countryside into the fantastical world of her creations: a world where frogs fish with a pole and bait, where mice are tailors, and where a small naughty rabbit will always sneak into a neighbor's garden.

Pamela Zagarenski

When I was a little girl, we would frequently visit my aunt in Concord, Massachusetts. I still remember the day I discovered this remarkable set of tiny green-spined books on the bookshelf in my cousin's bedroom. Beatrix Potter—she was both the author and illustrator. Immediately I was inspired. I had always known what I wanted to be, but with this new find I also knew who I wanted to be when I grew up.

It was never so much one single character or a single story. (But of course, there is always the endearing Peter Rabbit.) For me, it was the creator herself that I loved because I knew that she was, in fact, all of these stories.

While I painted these characters in celebration of Beatrix Potter's life, I could not help but think about how much she loved them. About how much they must miss each other. About how lucky for all of us that these stories were born of their remarkable mother, Beatrix Potter. And about how fortunate I feel to be able to honor her today for inspiring me.

Mr. Tod

Jemima Puddle-duck

Peter rabbit

Mrs. Tittlemouse

1866

Little Benjamin

HAVE MADE MANY BOOKS

I am going to make a story

THE TALE OF PETER Rabbit

I HAVE MADE MANY BOOKS

Beatrix Potter

The rabbits

I am going to make a story

For Beatrix